Seekers of the AWETO

I was born in Qinghai, a province in the western part of China, and the culture of that region has always been dear to me. I have carried it with me wherever I go, though over time, it has almost completely disappeared. I hope that this story, with its air of mystery, will inspire readers all over the world to find out more about my native land.

My thanks to all those who contributed to the original edition of this book: my dear friend Nicolas Grivel, my staunch supporter Mr. Wang Ning, translator Zhao Qingyuan and, above all, my wife, who always had faith in me and was there right from the start.

—Nie Jun

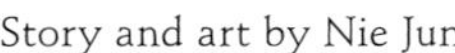

Story and art by Nie Jun

English-language translation by Edward Gauvin, with reference to the French translation and the original Chinese text

First American edition published in 2021 by Graphic Universe™
Published in arrangement with Gallimard Jeunesse and Sylvain Coissard Agency
Gallimard Jeunesse edition, *La chasse est ouverte*, published in arrangement with Beijing Total Vision and Nicolas Grivel Agency. *La chasse est ouverte* translated from the Chinese text by Zhao Qingyuan and Nicolas Grivel.

Graphic Universe™
An imprint of Lerner Publishing Group, Inc.
241 First Avenue North
Minneapolis, MN 55401 USA

For reading levels and more information, look up this title at www.lernerbooks.com.

Additional image (dot) by Stefy90/Shutterstock.com.

Main body text set in Andy Std. Typeface provided by Monotype Typography.

Library of Congress Cataloging-in-Publication Data

Names: Jun, Nie, 1975– author, artist. | Gauvin, Edward, translator.
Title: The hunt is on / Nie Jun ; translated by Edward Gauvin.
Other titles: Chasse est ouverte. English
Description: First American edition. | Minneapolis : Graphic Universe, 2021. | Series: Seekers of the Aweto ; Book 1 | Audience: Ages 12–18 | Audience: Grades 7–9 | Summary: "Xinyue and his brother are seekers, hunting Aweto—a rare, plantlike treasure—along the Silk Road. When Xinyue discovers the child of a deity that creates Aweto, it disrupts his already turbulent life." —Provided by publisher.
Identifiers: LCCN 2020020624 (print) | LCCN 2020020625 (ebook) | ISBN 9781541597846 (library binding) | ISBN 9781728420219 (paperback) | ISBN 9781728417493 (ebook)
Subjects: LCSH: Graphic novels. | CYAC: Graphic novels. | Fantasy. | Hunting—Fiction.
Classification: LCC PZ7.7.J83 Hu 2021 (print) | LCC PZ7.7.J83 (ebook) | DDC 741.5/973—dc23

LC record available at https://lccn.loc.gov/2020020624
LC ebook record available at https://lccn.loc.gov/2020020625

Manufactured in the United States of America
1-47924-48369-8/28/2020

第一部 大地的追獵

On the legendary Silk Road, there appears a growth with rare medicinal powers: aweto. Resembling a plant in summer and a worm in winter, it can heal any ailment under the sun. It is the name on everyone's lips, the dream of the rich and powerful—from nobles at their royal court to merchants the world over. Its trade has even created a curious profession: the aweto seeker. But rare as aweto is, there exists a breed even rarer: the celestial aweto. And whosoever finds it shall have eternal life . . .

Huh?

A swarm of insects! Almost as if…

Master, do aweto seekers really exist?

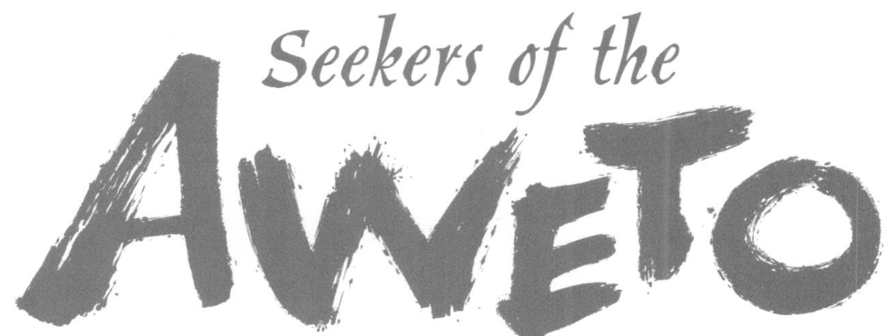

1. The Hunt Is On

NIE JUN

Translated by Edward Gauvin

Graphic Universe™ • Minneapolis

Indeed! Much mystery surrounds them, but everyone knows they have special gifts.

So it's true! I'd love to know more!

Once upon a time, in a western territory not far from the ancient Silk Road, there lived a mother and her two sons, drifting like vagabonds through the great desert.
Day and night they wandered, without destination, with only insects to guide them.

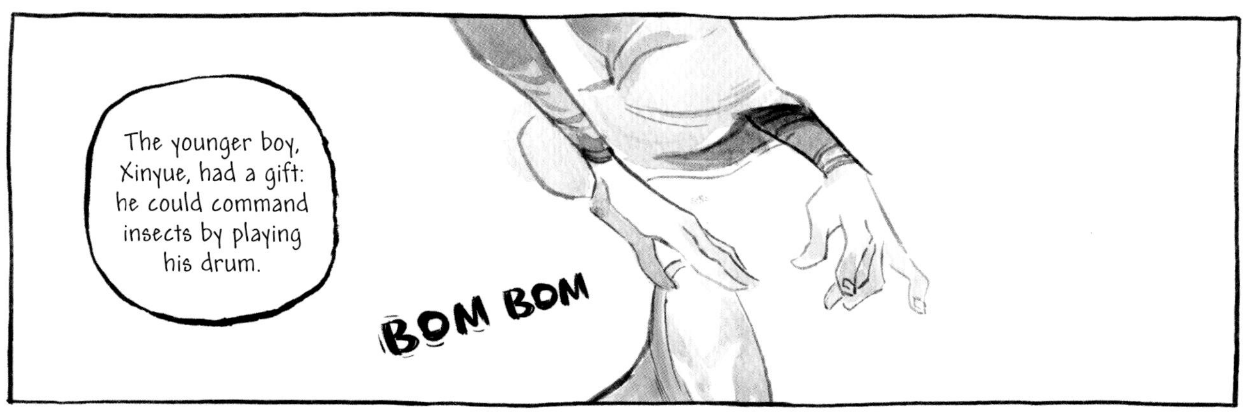

His elder brother was named Qiliu, and their mother, Bu Ren Niang. They were seekers of the aweto.

bom bom

Xinyue: new moon; *Qiliu*: drifting rider;
Bu Ren Niang: never apart

chadolos: colorful earth deities. The aweto grows on their heads, and an aweto is rumored to contain the soul of its chadolo.

That must be a Sanamo tribe. They're matriarchal.

Ashmi!

Huoxun: looking for the fire of survival

Invaders are approaching!

I'll handle them! Warn Our Lady!

Bzzzz

Bzzzz !

bom
bom
bom

bom bom
bom bom
The south wind is rising. Time to light a fire!

The aweto seekers are on their way! Flee! Men and livestock—into the mountains!

Bom Bom...

Bom...

What do the invaders look like?
It's that seeker who travels with a horde of insects. Watch out!
Oh no!
Our chadolo is about to give birth. We must protect her!
Understood, My Lady. They won't get through. We'll hold the line!

Our tribe is still recovering from the last few battles. I pray we can win this one.

In the face of such a threat, we must come together…

May our chadolo protect us!

How many arrows do we have on hand?
There aren't many left. But we'll make them count!

This is the worst possible moment for an attack.
They don't look like a large party. We'll fend them off!
Have you forgotten their insects, Ashmi? Don't underestimate them!
BZZZZz
Watch out for those young Sanamo women! They aren't allowed to marry till they've slain an enemy.
Hah! I'm just spoiling for a fight!
Hmph.

Wait for me, big brother!

Remember— I want lots of hot peppers in those noodles!

Qiliu, are you sure the celestial aweto really exists?
Of course!

...And to stay by your side, of course, big brother!

Enough! Now hang on.

Aim for the red-haired one!

FIUU!

Think that'll scare us off? Think again!
BLAM!
BLAM!

Ow! That hurts!

What's that old fool think she's doing?

POW

I see what Mama
meant about the
local customs...
Hey, look over
there!
Stand aside!

I just know there's some aweto around here!

FIUU!

Here's your welcome gift, seekers...

Flop!

Big brother!

We're almost there!

Right here!

Ahhh!

I'm close!

Look, Qiliu! Got it!

Watch out!

Let's get out of here!
This one must be gigantic!

Our chadolo!

WOMP
WOMP
WOMP
She's stirring!

Run for it! Now!

Oh no!

I've never seen a chadolo so huge! Why, it must be 100 years old!

Please! I'm begging you! Don't leave us!

Look! Our insects are heading back toward the chadolo!

Let's get out of here! She's starting to turn into quicksand!
Let me go!

Inside... the chadolo's child...
Forget it! We're too late...

She's already gone.

I'll get to the bottom of this!

Yue!

Wha—!?

AGH!

You hurt,
big brother?

That girl again!

Qiliu! Let's just leave!

Die, seekers!

Ah, you never listen to me!

She's gone too far!

Dirty thief! Give it back!

Give us back our aweto!
Fate has decided otherwise!

Huh?!

Oof!

Aaaaah!

Cough!
Cough!

Sniff

Mmmh!

Well, well!
A baby chadolo?
Hidden here?
That's a surprise.

Hey! No! I don't want any kisses!
Paaaa! Paaa!

Oh, you're way too affectionate for me!

I'll boil you and mash you!
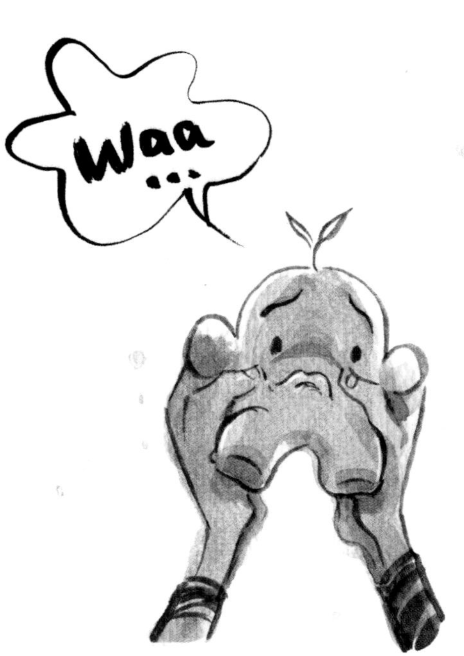
Waa ...

Waaaa!

Waaaaa! Waa!
Will you quit crying already?
...aaaaaa...

Helllp!

Big brother!

Sniff Sniff

Oh no!

Oww!

FLOP...

Oooh . . .

earthen tongue: a lost dialect unique to inhabitants of this region

What? You want **me** to look after your baby?

No! Don't go!
Why are you leaving
him with me?

It's that seeker's fault! Stealing the aweto killed our chadolo!

May demons take him!

When they grow up, the animal instinct awakens. They slay even their loved ones…

I said shut up!!

tian: sky; *zhao*: swamp

Guess you're not getting married just yet, Sanamo girl.

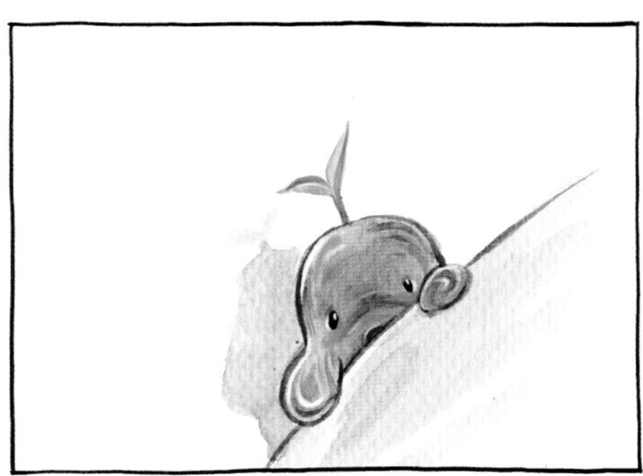

Stop! Who are you?

My mother says I have no country. I'm a son of the earth!

My name's Xinyue. If we ever see you again, I'll make you try some candied plum suckers!

So long, lovely sister of the bow!

: goodbye

You disappeared for a bit. Find anything?

Huh? Who, me? Nah...

Children! You're back at last!

So, hypothetically speaking... what if I found a **baby** chadolo?

Oh, a baby wouldn't be worth anything. Best to leave it behind.

Best to stomp it right then and there.
But I've always wanted a pet! Something cute and...

Don't be ridiculous!
I wonder if you're not hiding something...

Nope! Just asking! 'Scuse me! Nature calls!

Now what? Not that their reactions surprised me...

MmH?

Well... I guess this is goodbye.

See ya!

Paaa?

Bzzzzz

Ashmi!

Princess Huoxun.

I'm sorry. I couldn't protect our chadolo...
Our Lady says this was our destiny. At least you're not hurt!

Our pastures and our livestock are dwindling...
Those accursed aweto seekers!
Sniff, sniff, sniff
My Lady! You must punish me!
Oh, no, Ashmi. You are not to blame. We did what we could, but our defenses were too weak.
We were fated to pay for what our tribe did in the past. We had a debt to be settled.
How much time... do we have left?

When wolf ravagers attacked our land, the survivors fled with Princess Huoxun. The spirit of the earth accepted us and gave us fertile fields and ample water, letting hope blossom anew.

Take heart! It's still alive!

...

That young aweto seeker has it!

He didn't kill it either. We can still get it back!

I'll find that young seeker. The one who speaks the earthen tongue . . .

Go, my child!

Go, for the glory of our ancestors and the fate of our tribe! Take Nu and Mahn with you, and be careful. These lands are perilous.
My Lady . . . pray for us.

Princess, we can't! A hard road awaits us, and you're the Sanamo tribe's sole heir.

Don't underestimate me! Take me—please!

Stay here and look after Our Lady! We'll be back soon...

ZZZZZ

Paaa?
Pa?

You again?! What are you doing here?

Waaaa!

Shh!
Whatever you do, don't cry!

Are you trying to get yourself killed? If they find you, we've both had it!

You little pest! Stop clinging to me!

Go away! As far away as you can!

I should've ditched you first thing!

I don't want to see you again!

CAWWW

Oh no!

CRACK!

Where'd he go?

MMH...

No choice, I guess. Gotta keep you.
Do you know who I am? Or where I'm from? Wanna hear about it?
OOH!
I don't remember much about being a kid. I think I was born far, far from here...
But with gifts. Not everyone has them. I can speak the earthen tongue and command insects with my drum.

My big brother—he's the person I admire most in all the world.
It's not like we wanted to become aweto seekers. I don't enjoy it much. But we had to make a living somehow.
...Though I did enjoy candied plum suckers whenever Qiliu could steal them.
But as he grew up, he started getting obsessed with this one idea...
The celestial aweto! I have to find it!
The celestial aweto...

Since that day, we've sought an aweto from every tribe we come across. That's all we ever do as seekers.
My life has become a real nightmare. When I remember the scared faces of the poor folk we terrorize . . .
All that, and no one knows if the celestial aweto is even real! If eternal life is even possible!
ZZZZZ . . .
Ha ha!
Now I **have** to learn how to protec you, because . . . you're my first-eve friend!

I've heard of creatures like you. Half man, half animal...

...with red manes and eyes like a wild beast!

You talk too much!

The Tianzhao!

Aah!

What's this? Flowers!?
Cough!

Where'd this all come from?

My poor boy! Our aweto is drawing earthen magic to itself. It's making all the plants around us grow.

You had another nightmare, big brother.

Grrr!

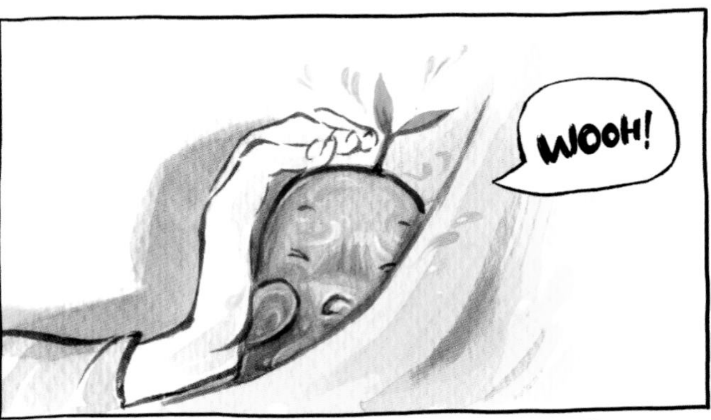

Don't forget, you have to get me some suckers once we reach the open market!

Hurry, boys. We still have a long way to go!

Look!

Who are *they?*
Must be the caravan of a princess of the capital, Can Tianjin ... maybe headed to a royal wedding!

Hmf!
I feel sullied by that young man's gaze!

Ooh! Her skin is as pale as fallen snow!

Koulun? Kill him!

Right! Wait, what?
No talking back, soldier!

Princess, we haven't the time to waste on those lowly aweto seekers.

A princess like that has never known life outside her luxurious palace. She must miss her family and her homeland, now that she's so far away...
Poor girl! How can she stand the desert heat?

Hey! I can see Yumen!

Open market, here we come!

Ashmi! Come look at this!
Only the power of an earth deity could work a miracle like that. The baby chadolo must have been here!
A field flowering in the middle of the desert!
Indeed! It proves he's still alive!

Those thieves must plan to sell the aweto at the open market. Let's catch them!
Yes!

No rest till Yumen!

Yumen is a border city and regional hub. A genuine crossroads on the Silk Road. The open market is held once a month to promote trade between merchants from all over the land. It is also a paradise for thieves looking to sell their loot.

Look! The first aweto seekers have arrived!

Quick, show us your harvest! We're ready to pay handsomely! Or fancy a good time with these two beauties?
Tee hee!

It's worth your while. Don't dither too long!
Houlmet! Watch your mouth. There are children present! If it's quality you're after, just stop by our stall. Bring your gold!

What could they have?
Goodness!

Those aweto seekers can be so disrespectful!
I must see for myself!

What's the matter?
Hmf!

Big brother, did you forget your promise?

Here!

Hee-hee! A stolen sucker tastes even sweeter!
Sigh.

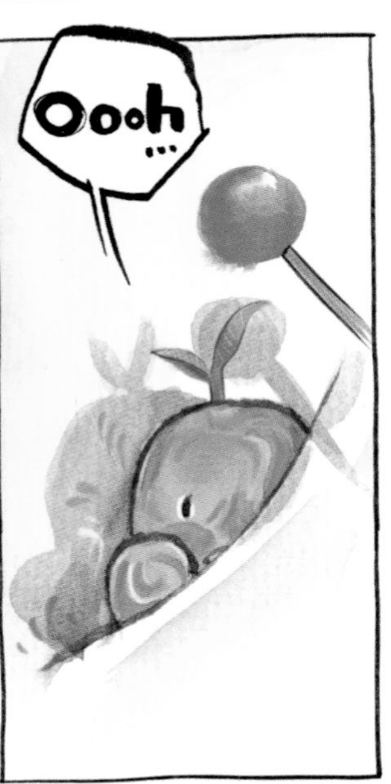
Oooh...

qiemi: attack with poison

Best not to turn our backs on that scum.

They give off that stench because they sleep in the sewer!

Croak

Hey!
Cut it out!

MMMH!

Where are you going!? Come back!

Stop!
Ha ha!

Big brother! I, uh, dropped something. Be right back!
Wha—?

Carefree as ever. Don't worry about him!

...

Hey! Watch it, kid!
Where'd he go?

Ooo? Paa?

Aaa!

Croak!

Sure you're seeing straight?

Nope. I'm real hungry. Lemme look again...

Where did that old hag go? Find her! Now!

I must reach her before anyone else does!

Ohhh! It is indeed a big aweto. But not of the highest quality...

A man of my experience can offer no more than fifty gold pieces!
And *you're* an official inspector of the emperor's goods and medications? You need your eyes checked!
Our starting price is 500 pieces!

bom bom bom bom
Cough!
Five hundred? You must be joking...

I'll give you 300 pieces, no more.
The drum! Xinyue must be in trouble.
Right!

Hey, tiny! Come back!

bom
bom

It's the boy who commands insects…

Don't you touch my friend!

Well, that's a new one. An aweto seeker, buddying up with a chadolo!

Bet you're waiting for it to get big, eh? Get a better price that way!

Croak!
bom
bom
bom
bom

Think you
can fool us just
like that?

You won't get
away so easily!

Slurp

Aah!

You're coming with us! Heh heh...

Huh? Aiee!!
Thwik!
Thwik!
Ah?

That's enough!

Ah! I-I've seen it...

I can die now!

What? What did you see?
The celestial...

...aweto!

What did he say?

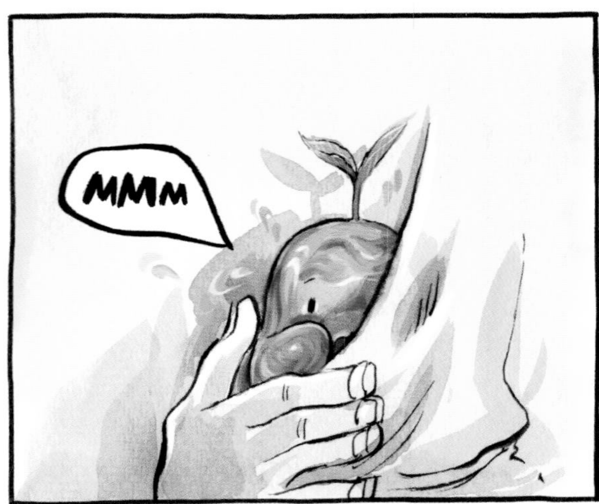
MMM

Well.

You found another chadolo, didn't you?
Spare him, big brother! Please!

Give it to me!
No! For once, Qiliu, let me choose!
bom

I want to protect him! I'm begging you!

My, how you've grown, Xinyue...

The boy who only ever cared about plum suckers...
TchK!

...wants a little more out of life.

You knew right from the start it was the celestial aweto, didn't you?
Him? **The celestial aweto?** What are you saying?

Qiliu! Are you crazy? That's your brother you're chasing!
Mama!

Out of my way! How dare you side with him!? You're not even real!

Not real? What are you saying? That I—I'm a... revenant?
Oh! I remember now!
Mama? You...
When a revenant wakes up, it turns into a cloud. You'll have to go now.
You look more like your father each day. Astonishing...
Where is he? I want to see him!
Oh no, no, no! I'll never tell! You mustn't!
Mama, what are you talking about!?

My time has ended now. But I'll still guide you from the heavens. I'll help you find your homeland.

What do you mean, Mama? My homeland?

I am not your birth mother. You are the son of the brave and good king of the old lands of Youzhi!
Youzhi?
Yes. The people there speak the earthen tongue. They live near the beautiful Pulei Sea, beneath Mount Sumeru. Go back to them, my child…

Get a hold of yourself. Our family was an illusion. The only real truth is the blood in your veins.

Sniff, sniff... I don't believe you! You're lying!

Open your eyes. We're not brothers by blood. Just a pair of aweto seekers with the same goal.

Now admit it! You've always wanted the celestial aweto for yourself!

But the celestial aweto is mine. **Mine!** I'll kill anyone who dares touch it! Understand?
You're wrong, big brother.

I don't believe...

Xin-yue...

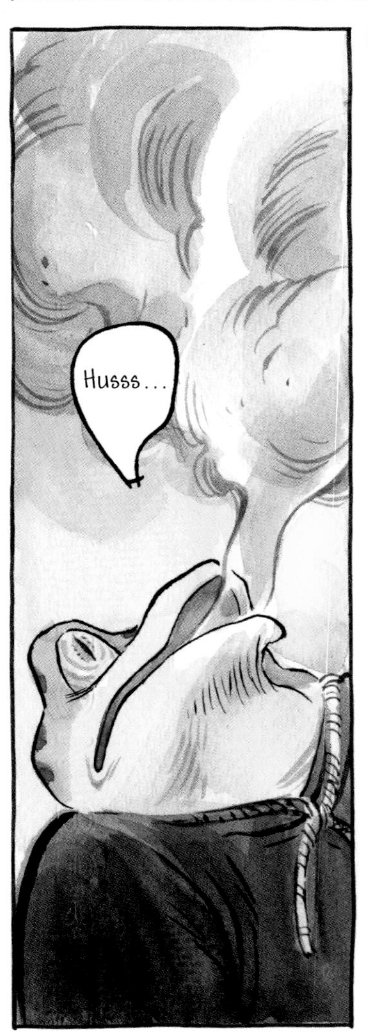
Husss...

Croak! The celestial aweto!

No one else will have it…

Look, those seekers are fighting! Seize this chance to arrest them!

The young royal here could be useful... I'll take him!
As for you, my boy...
If I can't finish you off, one day I'll pour your melted soul into the boiling sea and let you suffer there!
Stop!!

But I—I... cough, cough...

Farewell, boy of long-forgotten homeland
Once we find it, we'll be able to buy anything we want across the whole land!
Really, big brother?

Farewell, wretched seekers of all lands
Oh, Mother... Oh, my brother...

Sing a song of life along our journey

Until our salvation is at hand

Oh...

Whaat...?

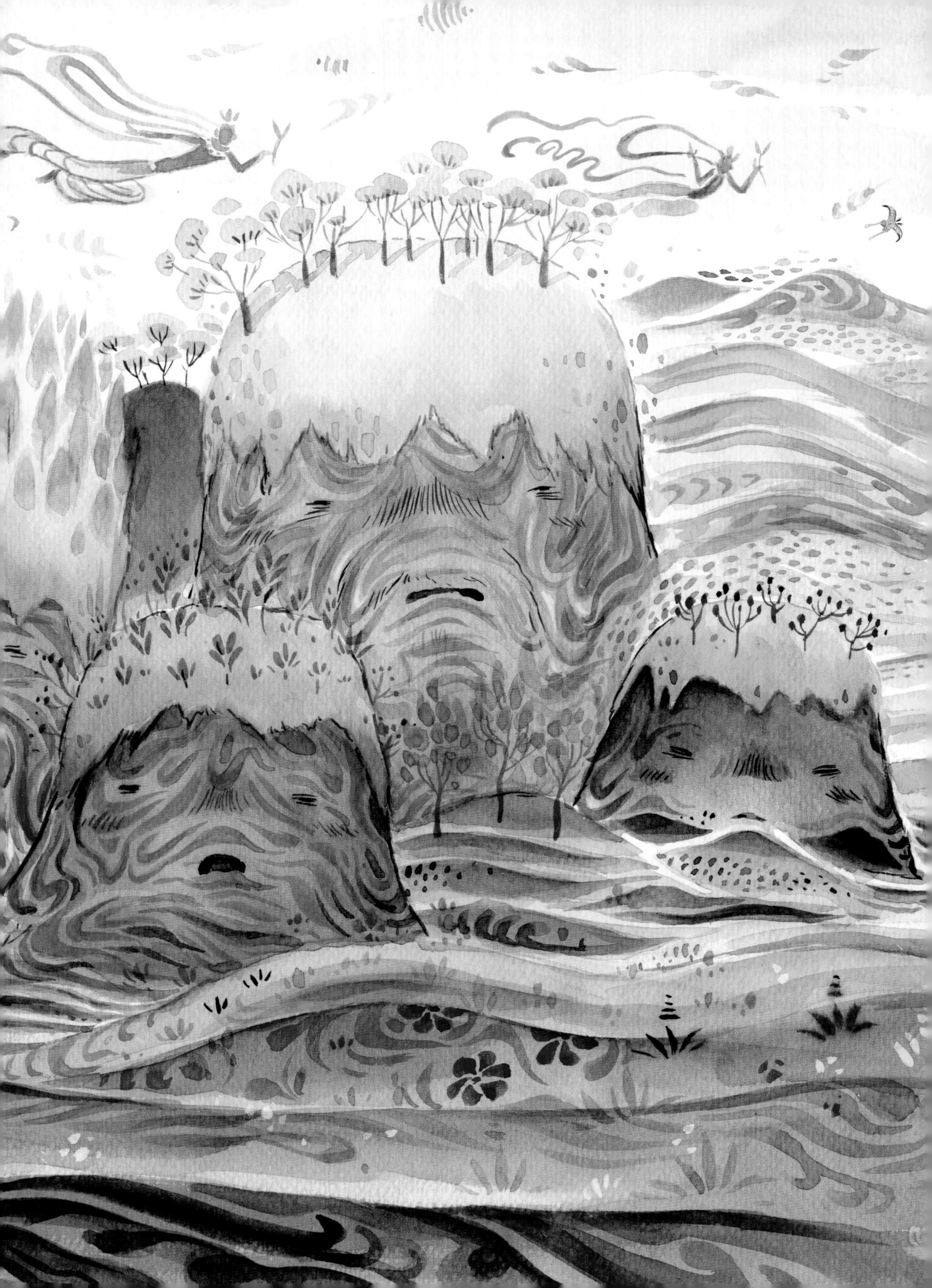

Forgive me!
I'm really sorry! For everything I did while I was seeking! S-stay back...

AWETO

To be continued…

The Land of the Aweto Seekers

Warm Sea

Great Blue Mountain

Mount Sumeru

Western Sea

Europe and the West

Huoxun Lands

Qiushe

Suye

Youzhi Lands

Pulei Sea

Qiemi Lands

Dayi Lands

Shendu Lands (India)

Land of the One-Eyed Men

Nanfu

Path of the principal characters